The Little Boy's Christmas Gift

The Little Boy's Christmas Gift

by JOHN SPEIRS

HARRY N. ABRAMS, INC., PUBLISHERS

In the East, long ago, a young boy helped his father to tend the gardens of three exceedingly learned men, Balthazar, Caspar, and Melchior.

When he was not needed by his father to work among the trees and flowers, the boy would learn from these great men as they studied together the history of man, the world around them, and the stars above. They were indeed the wisest of men.

One sparkling, clear night a new star appeared in the sky—bigger, brighter, and more beautiful than any they had ever seen before. The wise men knew its meaning at once.

"A great king is to be born!" they cried.

et us take gifts to celebrate his birth. Make haste! We will follow the star. It will surely lead us to him."

"May I come with you?" cried the boy. "May I come with you to meet the new king?"

"No," replied the wise men. "You are too young to make such a journey, and you have no gift fit for a king."

The wise men gathered together their most precious gifts and packed their camels with caskets of gold, frankincense, and myrrh.

And so their journey began . . .

The wise men moved off with their richly laden camels, following the star that shone both day and night.

Nobody noticed the boy with a small brown sack watching them.

After many days in the desert, they came upon nomads
    resting in their bright woven tents.

"Where are you going?" asked the nomads.

"We bear gifts for a new king," answered the wise men.
    "We follow that star to his birthplace."

"Then we shall come, too," said the nomads. "We will
    bring our best rugs so that he may never be cold."

And so they journeyed on . . .

The wise men with their richly laden camels
    and the nomads with their bright woven rugs.

Nobody noticed the boy with a small brown sack
    trudging along behind them in the dust and shadows.

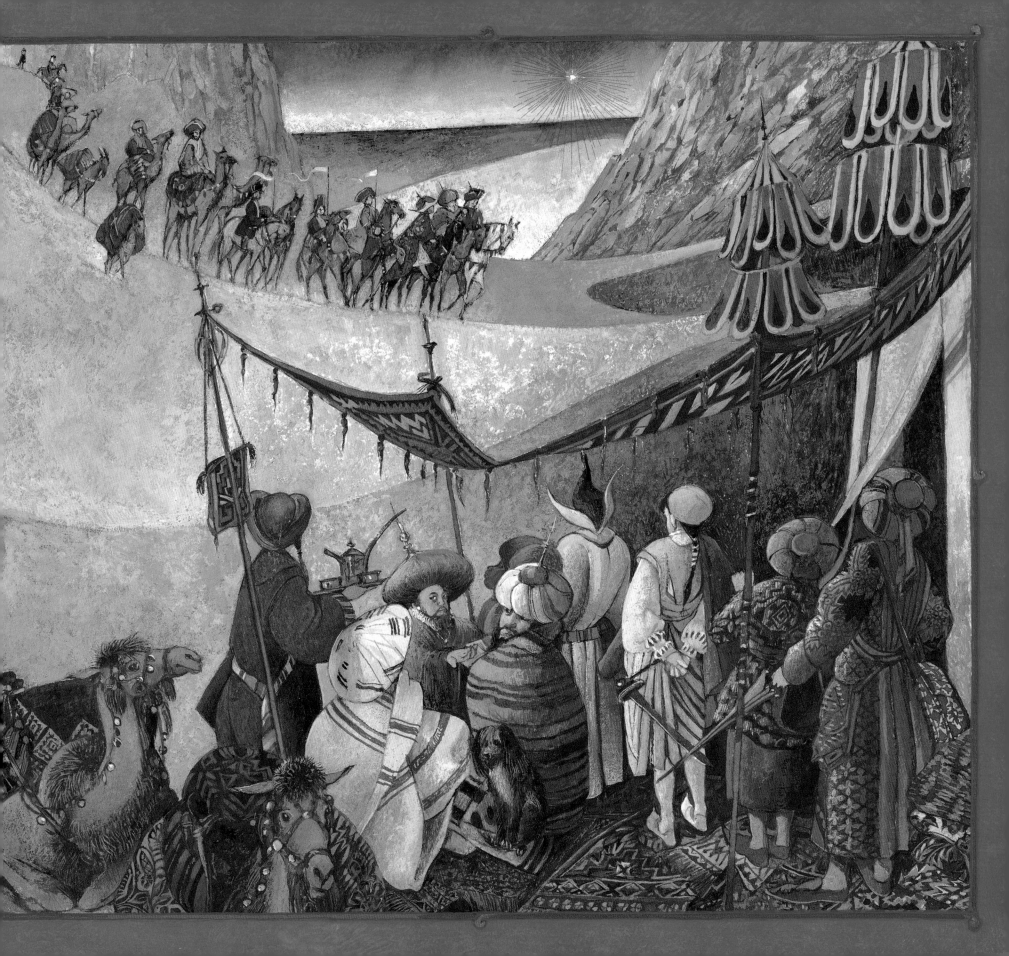

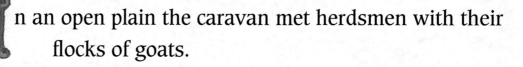

n an open plain the caravan met herdsmen with their
    flocks of goats.

"Where are you going?" asked the herdsmen.

"We bear gifts for a new king," answered the wise men.
    "We follow that star to his birthplace."

"Then we shall come, too," said the herdsmen. "We will
    bring our goats to provide fresh milk so the new king
    may never thirst."

And so they journeyed on . . .

The wise men with their richly laden camels,
    the nomads with their bright woven rugs,
    and the herdsmen with their goats.

Nobody noticed the boy with a small brown sack
    trudging along behind them in the dust and shadows.

The caravan stopped at a fertile grove where men were harvesting olives.

"Where are you going?" asked the olive growers.

"We bear gifts for a new king," answered the wise men. "We follow that star to his birthplace."

"Then we shall come, too," said the olive growers. "We will bring jars of our best olive oil so that the new king may always have light."

And so they journeyed on . . .

The wise men with their richly laden camels,
     the nomads with their bright woven rugs,
     the herdsmen with their goats,
     and the olive growers with their jars of oil.

Nobody noticed the boy with a small brown sack
     trudging along behind them in the dust and shadows.

After a time the travelers came to a valley where farmers
were gathering their crops of wheat, walnuts, and dates.

"Where are you going?" asked the farmers.

"We bear gifts for a new king," answered the wise men.
"We follow that star to his birthplace."

"Then we shall come, too," said the farmers. "We will
bring loaves of date and walnut bread so that the new
king may never grow hungry."

And so they journeyed on . . .

The wise men with their richly laden camels,
the nomads with their bright woven rugs,
the herdsmen with their goats,
the olive growers with their jars of oil,
and the farmers with their loaves of bread.

Nobody noticed the boy with a small brown sack
trudging along behind them in the dust and shadows.

They came to the outskirts of a town where beekeepers were tending the hives.

"Where are you going?" asked the beekeepers.

"We bear gifts for a new king," answered the wise men. "We follow that star to his birthplace."

"Then we shall come, too," said the beekeepers. "We will bring honey so that his life may be sweet."

And so they journeyed on . . .

The wise men with their richly laden camels,
    the nomads with their bright woven rugs,
    the herdsmen with their goats,
    the olive growers with their jars of oil,
    the farmers with their loaves of bread,
    and the beekeepers with their combs of sweetest honey.

Nobody noticed the boy with a small brown sack
    trudging along behind them in the dust and shadows.

long the way they were joined by musicians.

"Where are you going?" asked the musicians.

"We bear gifts for a new king," answered the wise men. "We follow that star to his birthplace."

"Then we shall come, too," said the musicians. "We will play for him so that his life may be filled with music."

And so they journeyed on . . .

The wise men with their richly laden camels,
the nomads with their bright woven rugs,
the herdsmen with their goats,
the olive growers with their jars of oil,
the farmers with their loaves of bread,
the beekeepers with their combs of sweetest honey,
and the musicians playing their bells, pipes, and drums.

Nobody noticed the boy with a small brown sack
trudging along behind them in the dust and shadows.

resently they came to a fork in the road. There they met shepherds.

"Where are you going?" asked the wise men.

"An angel told us of the birth of a new king," answered the shepherds. "We follow that star to his birthplace. We are bringing him two white lambs so that he may, in time, have flocks of his own."

"Then let us go together," said the wise men.

And so they journeyed on . . .

The shepherds with their two white lambs led the way.

The wise men followed with their richly laden camels,
    the nomads with their bright woven rugs,
    the herdsmen with their goats,
    the olive growers with their jars of oil,
    the farmers with their loaves of bread,
    the beekeepers with their combs of sweetest honey,
    and the musicians playing their bells, pipes, and drums.

And still nobody noticed the boy with a small brown sack
    trudging along behind them in the dust and shadows.

The star shone its brilliant light on a humble stable.

Inside they found a baby lying in his mother's arms,
just as the angel had told the shepherds.

The travelers knelt before the newborn child and gave to him their gifts.

The shepherds gave him two white lambs.

The wise men gave their caskets of gold, frankincense, and myrrh.

The nomads gave their bright woven rugs.

The herdsmen gave gourds of fresh milk.

The olive growers gave jars of oil.

The farmers gave loaves of bread.

The beekeepers gave combs of sweetest honey.

The musicians, on their bells, pipes, and drums, played the loveliest lullaby they knew.

The baby lay quietly in his mother's arms.

Then all at once, it seemed, everyone noticed the boy with a small brown sack, stepping out of the dust and shadows.

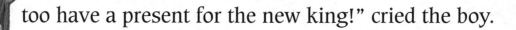

"I too have a present for the new king!" cried the boy.

He laid the small brown sack before the mother and child. Reaching inside it, he carefully pulled out a tiny tree.

"It's just a tree!" A startled whisper echoed around the stable.

"But look how he has decorated it!" said Balthazar.

"Look! Golden bunches of herbs and spices are tied with threads from the nomads' rugs!" said Melchior.

"Look how he has strung silvery goat hair with walnuts and shiny dates, green and purple olives," cried Caspar.

The herdsmen, musicians, beekeepers, and shepherds pressed forward to see little bells tucked between the branches of the tree. A tiny star, made from golden beeswax, nestled in a cloud of finest lamb's fleece right at the very top.

The boy offered the tiny tree to the baby.

The baby leaned forward and reached out his hands to touch it.

The star above glowed brighter and brighter.

The heavens turned to gold with choirs of angels.

All the people fell to their knees in awe.

The baby turned to the boy and gave to him the happiest of smiles.

The little boy, the gardener's child, was filled with such wonder and joy. For at that moment he knew that he had been blessed . . .

With the greatest gift of all.

DESIGNER: Darilyn Lowe Carnes

The illustrations for this book were painted on watercolor paper
in a mix of mediums, including watercolor, gouache,
varnishes, and oil colors.

Library of Congress Cataloging-in-Publication Data

Speirs, John
The little boy's Christmas gift / John Speirs.
p. cm.
Summary: A boy follows three wise men on their visit
to see the newborn Christ child
and presents him with a special tree as a gift.
ISBN 0–8109–4399–9
1. Jesus Christ—Nativity—Juvenile Literature. [1. Jesus Christ—
Nativity—Fiction. 2. Gifts—Fiction. 3. Christmas trees—Fiction.
4. Christmas—Fiction.] I. Title.
PZ7.S7468 Li 2001   [E]–dc21   00–051081

Published in 2001 by Harry N. Abrams, Incorporated, New York

Printed and bound in Singapore
10 9 8 7 6 5 4 3

Harry N. Abrams, Inc.
100 Fifth Avenue
New York, N.Y. 10011
www.abramsbooks.com

Author's Note

The main inspiration for the paintings that illustrate *The Little Boy's Christmas Gift* was the art of Northern Europe in the fifteenth and sixteenth centuries—the altarpieces of Jan van Eyck and Rogier van der Weyden, *The Life of the Virgin* by Hans Memling, and the extraordinary depictions of people going about their everyday lives in the paintings of Pieter Brueghel the Elder.

I conducted the research that culminated in the paintings for this book over a lifetime obsessed with the history of art, filled with visits to museums and galleries and countless hours poring over art books and catalogs.

In the fifteenth and sixteenth centuries, artists of Europe depicted Bible stories as set in their own times—incorporating contemporary clothing, buildings, and symbols. One such symbol—evergreens— had been used for centuries. Evergreens meant rebirth and renewal to the ancient Egyptians, Romans, and Druids. In the Middle Ages, religious plays re-created the Garden of Eden using an evergreen hung with red apples as its centerpiece. By 1521 in Alsace, fir trees were decorated with fruits and nuts, candles and paper flowers. Therefore, in the spirit of the artists who inspired me, I have used an evergreen as a gift from the boy to the Christ child. It is a symbol that will not be lost on today's children.

The original paintings for *The Little Boy's Christmas Gift,* which are only slightly larger than the printed page, were worked on heavy watercolor paper in my own mix of various mediums, including watercolor, gouache, varnishes, and oil colors, applied with very fine sable brushes.

It was very exciting to be given the opportunity to embellish the paintings with gold. I used it to enhance the angels and the Madonna and child, as artists of the period did, and on the text pages to emulate the richness of illuminated manuscripts.